To Martin and Jane, for bringing out the best in Mae, and me.

—Denise

❊

For my sweet Ayoub…
May your little wings help you get to where you want to be. May you stay curious
and open to all and everything; I will be right by your side all along the way.

—Maman

Text Copyright © 2020 Denise Brennan-Nelson
Illustration Copyright © 2020 Florence Weiser
Design Copyright © 2020 Sleeping Bear Press

All rights reserved. No part of this book may be reproduced in any manner
without the express written consent of the publisher, except in the case of brief
excerpts in critical reviews and articles. All inquiries should be addressed to:

SLEEPING BEAR PRESS™

2395 South Huron Parkway, Suite 200
Ann Arbor, MI 48104
www.sleepingbearpress.com

Printed and bound in the United States.

10 9 8 7 6 5 4 3 2 1

Library of Congress Cataloging-in-Publication Data

Names: Brennan-Nelson, Denise, author. | Weiser, Florence, illustrator.
Title: Mae the mayfly / by Denise Brennan-Nelson ; illustrated by Florence Weiser.
Description: Ann Arbor, Michigan : Sleeping Bear Press, [2020] | Audience:
Ages 4-8. | Summary: Soon after Mae the mayfly hatches she is nearly
eaten by a trout, sending her into hiding, but knowing she has only one
day to enjoy the world gives her courage to venture out again.
Identifiers: LCCN 2019047090 | ISBN 9781534110519 (hardcover)
Subjects: CYAC: Stories in rhyme. | Mayflies—Fiction. | Nature—Fiction.
Classification: LCC PZ8.3.B7457 Mae 2020 | DDC [E]—dc23
LC record available at https://lccn.loc.gov/2019047090

MAE the MAYFLY

By Denise Brennan-Nelson

Illustrated by Florence Weiser

Near the bank of the river one warm spring day,
a new life began, and her name was Mae.

Mama held Mae in a warm, tender hug,
then said goodbye to her sweet baby bug.

"You have your whole life—a day, perhaps more.
Don't waste it, Mae. Use your wings and explore!"

Her delicate wings were feathery light.
With a flit and a flutter, Mae took off in flight.

There was so much to see and so much to know,
but a dangerous thing was lurking below.

It was BIG.   It was HUNGRY.   It needed to EAT.

A newly hatched mayfly
would make a great treat.

Disguising its dark and deceitful sneer,
it pleasantly said, "Come closer, my dear."

"I have something here that you really must see.
But you're too far away. Come closer to me."

A voice inside her warned,

Mae, don't go.

But Mae didn't listen
and swooped down too low.

It sprang from the water
and that's when Mae saw
two rows of sharp teeth and a menacing jaw.
It snapped its mouth tight to gobble up Mae.

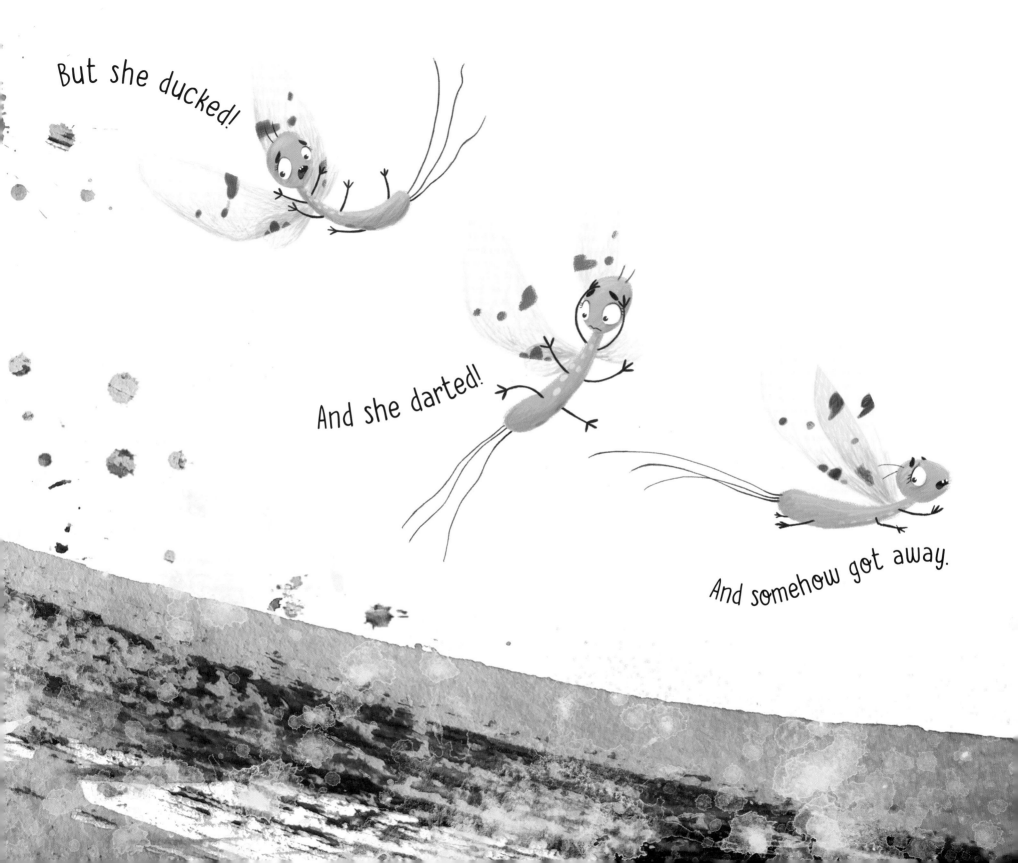

But she ducked!

And she darted!

And somehow got away.

Mae found safety in the hollow of a tree.
She covered her eyes and tried not to breathe.

Her body shuddered at the thought of Trout.

I'll stay here forever!
I'm not coming out!

But when her heart slowed, Mae heard a sweet sound.
Peeking out slowly,
she looked all around.

A robin nearby gave a cheerful tweet,
then flew to her babies with something to eat.

The mist on the river was a fine, pink cloak.
A bullfrog bellowed his morning croak.

Mae noticed the beauty of a web in the sun,
the glittering silk the spider had spun.

Mama was right—there's so much to see.
I can't live my life inside this tree.

So Mae launched herself from the dark, hollow place.
A greeting from the sun put a smile on her face.

Mae followed the river along as it flowed;
she saw cattails swaying and a stubby toad.

And bounding along without a care,
two cubs following Mama Bear.

There were bluebells in clusters offering up,
for Hummingbird, a cool drink from their cups.

A newborn fawn on wobbly knees,
and then in a clearing . . .
Mae could see . . .

a singing, dancing **jamboree** . . .

. . . a wild mayfly **jubilee!**

Joining in, Mae danced with glee!

The day rambled on and shadows grew long.
Nature was singing its afternoon song.

Mae floated along on a warm, gentle breeze . . .
when, faintly, she heard a desperate plea.

With shaky wings she followed the sound—
but Mae stopped cold at what she found.

Snagged in a mess, his body still,
the only movement from his gill.

Mae inched closer,
slow, unsure,
afraid again he'd lunge at her.

But Trout was weak, no flip or flail.
Tangled line had caught his tail.

Mae's eyes lingered on Trout's jaw.
But this time, there was more she saw.

The snag had taken all Trout's fight,
yet his colors shimmered in the light . . .

rainbow stripes in every hue:
silver, pink, and shades of blue.

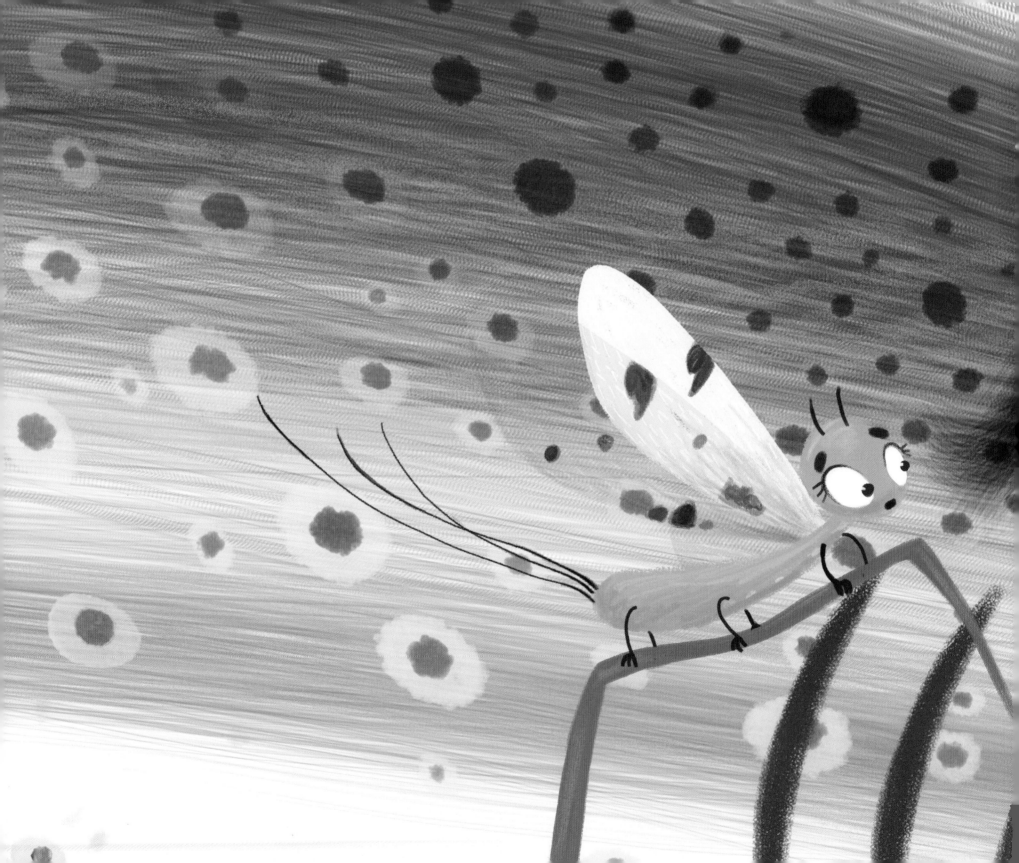

Mae saw a scar where once he'd fought
to keep himself from being caught.

And when her gaze met Trout's scared eyes,
We're not so different,
Mae then realized.

The fear she had felt, Mae now forgot
and she quickly started on the knot.

The knot so tight . . .

her progress slow . . .

but then . . .   at last . . .

the line let go.

The river carried Trout away.
Mae wondered, Will he be okay?

The silence was broken with a startling splash.
Scanning the river, Mae saw a flash . . .

. . . breaking the surface and catching the light,
Trout flipped his tail and waved good night.

And then an echo on the wind that blew,
two simple, precious words:

THANK YOU.

Her spirits matching the river's glow,
Mae settled in for the nighttime show.

Crickets and bullfrogs played their sweet tune,
while fireflies twinkled beneath the full moon.

The stars came out early for sweet little Mae.
She counted each one . . .
then called it a day.

∽ THE END ∽

MAE'S MINDFUL MESSAGE

Our minds wander, chatter, and distract us. When they do, we may not fully experience or enjoy what we are doing in the *present* moment.

With patience and practice we can learn to recognize when our attention has wandered and bring it back to the present moment. Being aware of what is going on around us deepens our gratitude and appreciation for the beauty in everyday things. It can also help us deal with life's uncomfortable and challenging moments. When Mae finally let go of her fear and worry, she was able to experience every little thing her day had to offer.

When your thoughts are noisy or overwhelming, and you want to bring your awareness to the present moment, remember to breathe. Mindful breathing can help us be more attentive, aware, and calm.

TRY THIS

See the dandelion flower and puff on these pages? Use them to practice mindful breathing. Relax your body and place a hand on your belly. Breathe in deeply and smell the flower on this page. Then breathe out and pretend you're blowing the puff off the dandelion on the next page. Notice the rise and fall of your belly as you breathe. Continue to bring your attention back to the breathing every time your mind wanders.

DID YOU KNOW?

- There are approximately 2,500 species of mayflies that can be found all over the world.

- The scientific name for mayfly is Ephemeroptera. This comes from the Greek word ephemeros, meaning "short-lived."

- Mayflies have been around longer than dinosaurs—over 350 million years.

- Mayflies are sensitive to pollution and their presence can be an indicator of clean water.

- In the nymph stage, mayflies eat algae. Adult mayflies do not eat at all.

- There are three stages of development for a mayfly: egg, nymph, and adult.

- A mayfly's life cycle—from egg to adult—lasts about a year, but its adult life lasts approximately one day.